STARS AND SCARS

Global Poetry Library

Copyright © 2019 by Global Poetry Library

ISBN 978-1-64606-041-2

Global Poetry Library

ACKNOWLEDGEMENT

Global Poetry Library acknowledges and thanks all the writers who put down there pens to contribute to this Anthology. This Anthology could be pending without your contributions.

We would Like to thank Lewis Wamwanda for editing and compiling this Anthology of poems,

To The Founder of Global Poetry, Poet Simba and all the support staff, thank you.

DEDICATION

We dedicate this work to all book lovers

iv

Contributing Authors

1. Lewis Wamwanda
2. Ruth Jemjor
3. Ezekiel Immo
4. Rajani Sharma
5. Stanley Chemweno
6. Sahaj Sabharwal
7. Solomon Ang'ong'a
8. Jael Kemuma
9. Souvik Chakraborty
10. Ashok Chakravarthy Tholan
11. Cynthia Ouma
12. Faith Jerop
13. Mukwhana N. Agneta
14. Christine Maobe
15. Esther K. Andaye
16. Ncube Tafadzwa
17. Daisy Eripon

Table of Contents

MY BAD BIRD CAGED

Chirping here and there

Cooing now and then

Forgive my bad bird

It's all I got

For a penny, I got it

As a birthday present from grandpa

But grandma never liked my bird

Named it a bad bird

Now she bought an ugly cage

With rusty and old metals

That shingles and tingles

And caged my bad bird

My bad bird never cooes

I rarely see it chirping

I seldom see it eat

My caged bad bird

© Lewis Wamwanda

Psssst I NEED TO SEE A PSYCHIATRIST

It's just like the old days, time doesn't change anything

We were even not married, we were cheating

But still when I stand at my kitchen door

I see her cooking

Now my wife is pregnant again

And our firstborn is in kindergarten

Every time he comes home from school

He talks about this friend of his

And the name reminds me of her

Life sometimes is full of turn arounds

Now my wife wants to name our baby girl Maria

If this is not torture, then it's psychological
suicide

How will I deny this name

You see, I cannot explain this to her

I remember when we fought about Jayden's
name

Our firstborn baby boy

How can I tell her that Maria was my Ex-
girlfriend?

And that name makes me feel guilty

She will no that I was a cheat, yes a cheat

And not only any cheat, but I cheated on her

Maybe she will leave with Jayden

And with our unborn "Maria"

So, folks, I'm frying in my own pan

These are the consequences of my choices

Another "Maria" for life

I am soon going to write a will

I heard Maria, my ex girlfriend, is pregnant

I'm not sure if I'm responsible

Because the last night we were together

I remember not to taste her served honey

But still I don't remember for how long I refused
to take it

See, I am a loyal husband my wife

And a good father to my kids

But still, time never changes everything

Not in my situation

I don't believe in that saying either

Now the memories hunt me at night

And my wife is always happy in the morning

Telling of how I dreamt of Maria

And telling of how I kept talking

Confessing my love for Maria

How will I tell her it is Maria

And not our "Maria"

It will break her into small pieces

I know her, a fragile being

Folks, I need to see a psychiatrist.

©Lewis Wamwanda

YOUR SMILE; YOUR GREATEST ASSET

Your smile is your greatest asset

Like the dazzling sun in a rainy season

Or like an oasis in the middle of a desert

Or like the full moon at night

Beautifying the earth below

Your smile is your greatest asset

That breaks the strongest of mountains

And emptying the largest of oceans

That melts the strongest of hearts

And making men yearn for more

Like milk and honey, finger licking delicacy

Your smile, like a lone rose in lilies

Of which brave bees run for sweet nectar

Sucking from the dippest part

Your smile is your greatest asset

Your smile, that changes truth to lies

Anger to laughter, and sorrow to joy

That changes the alphabets,

From A to Z, to Z to A

Your smile is your asset.

©Lewis Wamwanda

GONE FOR A WHILE

I will let you go

For as long as you want

I won't hold you back

Because you promised you'll come back

And when you arrive at the front door

Check for the keys under the mat

I'll keep the knob oiled, to ease your work

And please, don't leave your shoes outside

Behind the wooden door

Are pink notes written with black ink

I can't tell you how many they are,

But depict from the days, months or years you'll
be out

On the reading table my love,

You'll find our favorite book

Flip through the pages,

There will be a surprise waiting

And I'll be in the bedroom

Entangled in your favorite sheets

With my eyes closed,

My breathe gone

And my body rotten

©Jemjor Ruth

GREENER PASTURES

The grass is greener on this side

 You members of the city

Why are you eating trash

And calling it digital food

When the fields are flourishing with all kinds of
food

Eaten when fresh and healthy?

The grass is greener on this side

Yee members off the city

Why do you kill and fight for women

With artificial figures and fake faces

Yet there are ripen angels, with beautiful hearts

Not so far, just here in the country side?

The grass is greener on this side

Yee members of the city

Why do you live in small houses

Equaling the size of a cattle shed

When there's abundance of space here,

That we even got room for mice?

The grass is greener on this side

Yee members of the city

Food is in abundance, surplus

Water is free, god given

Land and space is large too, no suffocation...

The countryside is a paradise on earth

©Jemjor Ruth

CHOICES

Watery eyes, clouded mind and heavy heart

A rope on the hand, decision made

Trodding down the lonely path

Deep into the forest, the favorite Mugumo tree

The place of skull, whence all could be finished

The steps became heavier, suspicions of being followed

Left, right, front, center , no one in sight

The mission should be accomplished, today or never

Three two one steps closer, bitter party almost beginning

But still, he felt under watch, invisible burning gaze

He set the stage so systematically,

Like Elijah during the mount Carmel contest

And when everything was due set, he bowed for the last prayer

There was rattling in the bushes

As he lifted his eyes, they met with hers

Pleading yet accusing eyes, he was shocked

"If you really do love me dad, don't do it" she cried out

Everything had to be undone, everything

A new start had to be done, for her only
daughter

©Jemjor Ruth

FATHER

You are behind every carefully checked step of my life,

Along with my mother who is your wife.

Without your help I was not able to work rife,

And my life would resemble cutting pebble with blunt knife.

Every step of mind is under the supervision of your eyes,

While taking decisions, you are so wise.

Following your advice ,

My performance subsequently rise.

You fulfilled every requirement of mine,

Even before it was demanded my cine.

You provided me healthy, delicious meal even before you dine,

For me you have made everything fine.

I am so glad,

By God's grace, to have such a great dad.

In your presence, no one can feel sad,

And what you want from me is just a tad.

Now it's time to make you feel proud,

That's all my inner voice saying so loud.

And also in a peaceful, royal place away from huge crowd,

After all, making a confidently, relaxed rout.

©Sahaj Sabharwal

TEACHER

Giving us knowledge of something is a teacher,

Having an inbuilt experience feature.

A good teacher teaches us by heart,

And prays God for our part.

A teacher helps us in developing our mind,

In such a way that is very kind.

A teacher teaches us tricks to achieve our goal,

And warns us to remain careful to avoid any

hole.

Without the help of a teacher, we cant work rife,

And many difficulties will appear in our life.

In this vast world, they are teachers and parents

only ,on whom we can rely,

They always keep on us their eye.

And we are confident that they never tell a lie,

They gives us blessings so that we can fly high.

That's why , Parents are our caretaker,

And teachers are our future maker.

©Sahaj Sabharwal

SILENCE

Silence

Its the only solace

When the potency of fighting is weakened

When the battle field is no longer visible

Due to the blood drained out from the eye

Silence

Is the only option

When words become meaningless

When speaking out means hurting others

And when any sound made chokes the throat

Silence

Is the only friend

That never judges for who someone is

But comforts in all faithfulness

And doesn't ask for anything in return

Silence

The only remedy

To the world that provokes repeatedly

That stabs countless knives from all directions

And never cares the damage it causes

Silence

My only option

My solace

My friend

And remedy

To the hostilities of the world

©Ruth Jemjor

I STILL REMEMBER

True to you Faith

Yours slightly taller height

Yours graceful gait

And a wow sight

Yours big, beautiful eyes

I'd say enchanting

My sapio-sexual self

Admired you brainy elf

Beautiful memories kept alive

So much to recall

Yet so little penable

Summary is impossible

There's an happy emotion

Just by abled communication

After so long, for long it's been

Just grateful to The Almighty

For keeping you safe and healthy

For allowing interaction

For long it's been, after so long

©Solomon Ang'ong'a

SWEET-HURT

With eyes focused at infinity

Sat quietly seemingly calm

But inside its rage, a turmoil

Rage or pity, or perhaps wounded

Should sooth the wound with palm oil?

She couldn't see me

All the efforts to zero

Proved am no hero

Everything turned vanity

From sweet nothings

To bitter hurting

The sweet-hearting

To heart-piercings

But affinity for love

Hasn't left me peaceful

I want her, her alone

It's the cry of a rejected soul

The fight too hard, dejected

Can I have a drink am exhausted?

No, I'd sing of her when drunk

So I summon little strength left

I'll steal her heart, call it theft

Persevere some more snobs

Turn the knobs

Unlocking doors to her heart

For my Love's sake

I'd stay a fighter

Ain't quitting without winning

©Solomon Ang'ong'a

HUMANITY

Considered as a curse

To purgatory she belongs, burning

Homeless and penniless

No medical attention paid

On streets she scratched

Hoping to rise to grace

She's a kleptomaniac

Standing one klick away

Staring at her like a site

Unwanted by the society

With sunk eyes she stares back

Stretching her pale hands for help

"Lack of humanity"

Tears rolling down her cheeks

In pain and at large flowing

Shivering in coldness

Multifarious stones thrown at her

Wicked minds full to capacity

No sympathy, `*"she deserves death*

Lack of humanity "

In pang she cries out loud

In pang I witnessed her death

Giving me sleepless nights

Distressful mind day after day

Not being able to help

Forever guilty featuring on my mind

©Jael Kemuma

PREGNANCY

Long awaited

With zeal

For decennary

Contempt, alluded as fruitless

Dissociated and abhorred

Overworked and thrashed mercilessly

Power of pregnancy

Exultation and consideration, gained

Tranquility and unity, invigorated

Love and care, flamed

Cage to mansion

Slave to queen

Unwanted to wanted

Power of pregnancy

©Jael Kemuma

FEMALE POWER

Not sorcery, call it power

Not ironical, call it power

Not falsehood, call it power

Strength of a woman

She is a being of love and care

She is the root to good-tortunt

She endures all sorts of throes

Strength of a woman

Through the toilsome world

Life knocks her down countlessly

Crying to the ground, picks herself up and

shakes of the dust

Strength of a woman

She is your weakness

One touch, repatriating you to extinct world

She is the root to your indemnification

Strength of a woman

She is who she is

In the name of love, she is woe-be gone

In the name of love, coming back to you

Brightening her days,

Strength of a woman

THE HIGH ROAD

Ubiquitous through the diurnal motions of a
rogue planet,

I stand tall, and stand high -

the moral compass gravitating forever to my
ascent.

A thousand denizens walk past -

some with dreams on their plate,

escalating my arduous steps on their own accord,

withered by storms cascading through mortal
veins.

Storms that are often too trivial and yet obscure,

sometimes ever grotesque.

Some travelers surge through my arduous paths -

unabated and yet tilted by dictates of time and
space,

some even fragmenting dreams along the way.

Often the storms plunder deep into the annals of
life,

causing casualties,

seeping some into the gorges of wilderness,

mystifying any miniscule chances of resumption.

Some never care to indulge in my escapade

and resort to casting aspersions on my very
sanctity.

Not all those who embark on my precipitous
path survive to see the glorious sunrise

at the weary end of the steps, where truth bears
no ties.

The high road is not a frivolous escapade,

nor an inane excuse of self-contentment.

The ever gruel between the facets of the mortal
mind is as ubiquitous as I am.

The diurnal choices between me and the rest
define an integral spoke of life -

uniting people, yet causing strife.

Taking the high road is not a choice nor a

compulsion -

rather the mere symbolism of the intricate

idiosyncrasies of the mind.

There's nothing to gain nor anything to lose.

And yet, my friend, what you shall certainly find

Is an ethereal lightness of being.

©Souvik Chakraborty

THE SOJOURN THROUGH MEMORIES

You're not a figment of my imagination,

nor the stuff made of dreams.

When the escapades of life come to a solemn

standstill,

or in restive times - times that seem to clutter in

deep,

shreds of the bygone moments often elusively

peek

into the undulating crevices of the frescoes of

time.

And then, I yearn, often ache, to delve

into the radiant realms on your ever-growing

territory,

seek solace from the scathing scruples of reality

-

slog through the fog shrouding your misty

entrance.

But alas, all I get is a palate of colors - the dark

and the bright.

The sentient mind pervades deep into it,

scouring for the sake of reminiscence.

The celluloid offers in a sneak to a myriad host

of moments,

unravels beings who once walked the path - this

very path -

some who never cared,

some who hated to the annals of hate, some who

loved an ethereal love -

same, yet different without them.

I extend my arms to touch, feel and take in

this very oblivious and apparent surrealism -

but alas, curse the cruel dictates of time.

Still, the window of the longing mind opens,

threatens to transcend the barriers of space and

time -

fills in the senses with your rendering essence.

And when, the dictates of time seep in,

reducing my access to mere symbolism,

all I get from you is a baffling assemblage of

lights, sound, and blurry imagery -

envisioning a well of depth - the depth of life.

Memories - you're all I shall ever have to take on

my way back,

defying time through your colored glass.

©Souvik Chakraborty

IN DEEP MISERY

The materialistic world is illusive,

Like a fly caught in the cobweb;

Tangled are we to the desires beehive

Where egoism holds us in a sweet garb.

Our attitude and inner-self actions,

Those harbor the zeal for pleasures;

Entice us with ever-new passions,

Forcing us to become slaves of desires.

Like a strong wind that easily extinguish

The very flame of a burning lamp;

Passions ignite wrath and anguish;

In deep misery they eventually dump.

Sin, error or evil, whatever we deem,

And the meritorious deeds we execute;

Only the God can weigh and redeem,

None can save use if demerits are acute.

©Ashok Chakravarthy Tholana

TO CHOOSE BETWIXT

Humanity is caught

Betwixt good and bad,

Betwixt devil and God,

Betwixt hope and desires,

Betwixt joy and distress,

Betwixt love and hate,

Betwixt luck and fate,

Betwixt worship and faith,

Betwixt life and death,

Betwixt mercy and cruelty,

Betwixt ugly and beauty,

Betwixt right and wrong,

Betwixt weak and strong,

Betwixt peace and violence,

Betwixt serenity and turbulence.

Encircled by clouds of desires

And losing the discriminate sense,

The bliss of self-vision gets spoilt

Betwixt hasty and turbulent acts.

How come then,

True wisdom prevail

To choose betwixt ….

Mortal and immortal faith;

The one that confers fleeting joy

The one that confers eternal joy?

©Ashok Chakravarthy Tholana

BELOW LIVES A LIFE.

The wind blows ,tall trees knock,

Dark clouds move in mountains' rings,

It rains with ice, clearing the blue sky

Then warmly it shines.

Mixed scents from the gardens,

The flowers blossom happily,

Results from the dry buried seeds,

The farmer's hopeful relief.

Careful, mind your steps,

Spare the crawling brothers,

Give ears to the crickets,

An icon of peace you shall remain.

The river flows with ease,

Breathing air refreshes,

Burning ground is cooled,

Every thirst is quenched.

To you, us, I pen this ,

A letter of love and a reminder it's,

Whatever you do, forget not,

"Below, lives a life."

©Cynthia Ouma

HALLOWEEN GHOSTS

Give me a wake up call,

It's early for my alarm,

My intestines are cold,

The strength is gone.

Weary from the day,

The dusk gave a rest,

Now back on the street,

Flew or swam in sleep?

Pumpkin humans!

How?

Scary faces .

Have you heard? Seen?

Darkness scares more.

But the moon is here,

Reflecting the mixed paints on the faces ,

Loud laughter and cries from every head.

Funny. Scary. Sad .

The faces after me.

Weak. Helpless.

I'm dragging on grounds. Hoping over blocks.

Boiled temperature .

Shivers and pants. Listen to the knocks,

Mixed voices of my name

Ooh my poor precious soul.

I'm wet and burning,

The Halloween's ghosts are here,

Loud drum beats. Cock crows, sharp and far

away,

Thank you. Thank you for saving my soul.

November wastes not time,

Hail you Friday!

©Cynthia Ouma

GRAVITY IS LOOSENING IT'S CLAWS

I am suffocating due to lack of attention

I am weighed down and hopeless

I am hopeless and invaded by ill thoughts

I feel there's no other way

Everything to me seem pitch black

I feel drowned in a deep depression

An weird idea bribes my mind

I feel to feed myself with a poisonous birthday

cake

As I pick a sharp knife

I sharpen it on my wrists

Ain't fit for this world anymore

The life's bliss is hard to be blown off

I can't go ahead to live a lie on the brink of death

I tie a noose

And as if that's not enough

I take a flight from a Cliff set high

Poseidon's realm pulls me down to it's depth

I embrace that last kiss though

But instead I kiss death ; I QUIT.

©Faith Jerop

HORNY DEMONS

They slowly creep into our fields

We try to run away but our speed cannot

supersede theirs

They have crooked legs with steady strides

They have long and curved horns

Huge hands that could even grab and steal the

whole village at once

I choose to watch at their fight with human

beings

With the first horn that's holed they strike

fiercely with hunger

It has in it thin beings with stunted growth

Whom you could at ease count the number of

ribs in their concertina chests

Not only that but also a raged war and slaughter

of own kids for consumption

The second horn that seemed to sting

Is made up of a corrupt world

Where leaders down troth their voters

They make them beggars on the roads and their

gates

They at times send guards to whip and send

them off

Bribe is the key propeller of survival

Who would cry for the poor and impoverished

The horn is too sharp to smart them deeply

The third and fourth horn are intertwined

They're made up of hate and identity

That if you belong to a certain social status

Hate and discrimination is fueled by your high

or lower caste

Most of whose identities are poor get a ticket to

be a face of hate

©Faith Jerop

MAMA'S FRIENDS

Mama has friends

Female friendly friends

Who're ever around her

At home,stream,market

Mama loves these mamas

They pour numerous notes

And uncountable presents

To mama and other mamas

These lovely mamas

Have made mama proud

Mama borrows none anything

Mama lacks nothing

But, mama's friends

Are not fair

They love mama, not papa

They love mama, not mama's children

They make mama

To harass papa

To give papa deaf ears

To despise papa

©Mukwhana N. Agneta

READING MY EULOGY

Caged in the casket,

Sobs from the gathering,

Dressed in black are my people,

Dressed in a white gown is me,

Caged in the casket, reading my eulogy.

Empty words they spit,

Those tears will dry by sunset,

Holding on to my picture in black,

Standing with a smile in white,

Watching them agonizing , reading my eulogy.

She's gone, too young for death,

Her art, dead souls re-igniting,

Her eyes, like pearls,

And I, laying in my casket,

Watch sand on my casket glass, reading my eulogy.

- 71

©Christine Maobe

(Chrismoh The Poet)

IF I NEVER SEE THE LIGHT OF DAY

If I never see the light of day,

Come closer to my cold body,

Kiss my forehead and let your tears drop on my eyes,

Cry as much as you can and scream my name,

Let me hear you in my second world,

Look at my palm incase I left a message,

Write one incase I didn't,

Put my picture in a frame and hang it on your wall,

Light a candle and let it burn on my chest till it fades,

Show them the pictures we took and share the memories we shared,

Narrate the stories I once told you and carry our secrets with you

Don't let our enemies see my body,

Cover me with a golden shawl,

If by chance you miss me,

Just close your eyes and remember the memories

worth cherishing,

Smile and let your heart cry,

I'll be gone but not from a heart that truly loved,

But when that happens,

Always remember I LOVED YOU.

©Christine Maobe

(Chrismoh the poet)

WATCHING OVER MY GRAVE

Hands on my knees,

By my grave I sit,

Watching at dusk,

Leaving at dawn,

Watching the growing rose,

On top of my grave,

My body lying down there,

And I'm watching over my grave,

They can't kill me again when I'm dead,

They already did,

That night on my way home.

©Christine Maobe

(Chrismoh The Poet)

THE HUNT

My clock screams 3am

My super hearing power is back

I can hear their loud cheers

They are almost here

My nose is not spared the smell of emptiness

Neither the smell of fresh blood

My mouth still has the sweet blood taste

They are back

It is time for the hunt!

My heart can't be contained anymore

It is threatening to break my ribcage

Ouch! Please heart!

Spare me today

Allow me to rest

I agreed to hunt yesterday

Use the energy that you obtain yesterday

Please! Be calm

Don't let them convince you

©Esther K. Andaye

I WOKE UP DEAD

I thought in death lies darkness

That in peace the dead rest

That there is another world for the living dead

But now I know better

I woke up dead

I woke up dead

Found my lifeless body lying peaceful

In a world I once lived

Maybe I am still alive

Maybe dead

Or maybe this state is the living dead

I am alive, I am dead

I am alive for I can walk

I feel not my heartbeat

But I believe I am breathing

I can talk better than ever before

But I am dead

I can talk but nobody can hear me

I am transparent for nobody sees me

My body is insensitive to touch

I need not a path to use

For I make way through barriers

Am I a ghost?

Or am I just blessed with supernatural powers?

I woke up dead

I believe I am alive

But I feel lifeless

Which state am I?

Somebody, please

Rescue my worried mind

Please assure me that I am alive

©Esther K. Andaye

One Final Shot

The breeze that blew on his face was charged with the aroma of past, tempting his sense to go back to the place where he belonged to. But it was too late; the time was gone, and with it the hope of going back had elapsed. He had chosen this life, to follow his passion over the blue-collar job his father had intended for him.

As the ship lurched its way through the waves of the ocean, he lay there squinting his eyes from the harsh sun rays watching a Seagull Soaring high up in the sky.

"It could be a perfect shot," he thought still laying there without moving a muscle. He wished he could have his hands on his weapon he could have got that bird's shot as a trophy. If only his hands were free from the knots he would grab his weapon for the perfect shot.

"It's time to say good bye, intruder" a man's voice was heard, who placed his gun point on the captives head.

"Any last wish?" he asked.

The captives nodded as he saw few more of the seagull diving back… "Oh! God one shot please.…" Was what he continuously prayed for, even at that crucial moment!

With his hands loosened and the cloth removed from his mouth he coughed hard and said in gasps" I want to Take a shot of that bird…"but before he could finish his words the gun went BANG and brought the bird fluttering down on the deck. …
" your wish is granted" the one eyed man said with the smoke still swirling out of the gun mouth. The captive's eyes widen with horror.… "What did you do? I wanted a shot…why did you kill it?" He said reaching out for the pouch tied on his waist.

With his hand still clung to something inside that pouch. "I did it for you" was the reply from the man with the gun, before the captive could pull out what his pouch had, "Bang" went the gun. With that the entire ocean went silent.

The captive was down with blood gushing out from his forehead and his hands glued to the camera in the pouch.

©Ragani Sharma

WHAT IS TIME?

"Time is a teacher, but unfortunately it kills its pupil" beautifully written on time but this line reminded me of few more proverbs outlining Time, 'Time is money', 'Time heals all wounds', 'Time is precious and cannot be bought' and many more. This makes it clear that people have their own view on time, as and how they experience it.

Time definitely is the best teacher as it brings Endurance, patience, maturity in every human life; transformation that every human goes through with the passing time, be it for their well or ill being.

If you are to take a stroll over the memory lane, which part would you like to relive all over again? Well, given a chance, most of us choose to go back to school or college's days, same old friends and the gala time spent together. Our thoughts and ideology were completely different then, filled with enthusiasm, ready to face whatever come may.

Our outlook of life now completely differs from what we thought of then. Our strategy to face the problems thrown to us by the world might not tally with our plans back then.

Why is it so? Same mind having different approach towards life and the situations we are put into.

I guess with passing time our perspective of life changes; in some cases it actually contradicts our own ideologies back then. We have developed patience in dealing with problems and have become thought full before indulging into any responsible deeds. It has definitely taught us Patience and endurance making us mature enough to face the world subtly.

Everything dies with time; it not only kills our physical being but even our dreams and aspirations, desires and our wishes. It puts us in such situations where we fail to remember what our dreams were what we aspired and wished for.

Lucky are those who got the opportunity to perceive their dreams and run after what they actually aspired for. Though the road towards it was not paved smooth and black topped, they actually had to carve their way out to their dreams.

It is not that time is always harsh on us. It brings many opportunities but we fail to recognize them or may have over looked them. Few of us are forced into wherever they are now, and few are here by choice or may be our decision gone wrong by the passing time(late realization.)

Whatever the reasons may be Time has a great role in shaping our life. When you get the chance make the most out of it, as it says "If you kill time you'll bury opportunity".

We need to realize that life is one time offer it neither waits nor comes back so we better use it well.

©Rajani Sharma

MY DEAREST

Mine, you are my dearest

Among all, you're my best

My star in the blue sky

To reach you, I must fly

In my arms you're secure

For my thoughts are pure

Forever you, I shall not lure

Trust me I assure

My heart is at peace

Only when you're at ease

Forever I will not cease

To love you is my please

© Ezekiel Immo

THE ROAD I LEFT BEHIND

Once I trod a beaten path

On a journey across the savanna

And zeroed in on a diversion

Crisscrossed two roads

Of the two I wondered

Which my destiny shall lead me

The rocky one, the grassy one

To which shall bring forth my destiny

I chose the rocky road

And trod like there was no diversion

Perhaps the other was the better

But who cares the lesser

In my head it was the right one

Or unless there was another day

My net to cast

And catch a new species of fish

For until then

My destiny shall be safely gripped in my palms

©Stanley Chemweno

THE DEMONS IN MY CLOSET

Last night I had noise from my closet

the ghosts of my past sneezed and whizzed

branding brand new scythes

to my shock and horror

they danced in the pitch of black

in no particular direction

I saw them

parading my favorite waistcoat

I saw them down my happy socks

in the windsock heads..

I saw them lashing themselves

carelessly with my buckle

two played fetch with my hat

another hushed them not to wake me up

while

yet another spoke in my ear

in eternal fear to be bound

below mounds to disappear

cringed in my bed I peeped

and saw them disappear

into dust

not so without a little note

on the inside of my closet

we shall be back for you

© Stanley Chemweno

FIND ME A FRIEND

Find me a friend

Who will be there in my defense

And save me from the deep end

And never my enemies to befriend

Find me a friend

A ride or die one so to say

High tides, low tides to stay

And never my wishes to sway

Find me a friend

To conquer the world with

Wielding swords of a blacksmith

Our adventures to trend like a myth

Find me a friend

To back up my secrets to the cloud

and stick by me like glue

tend to my flue

and stand me out from the crowd

Find me a friend

to enrich me with knowledge

not to say I went not to college

but to quench my thirst

that was otherwise submersed

©Stanely Chemweno

THE COMFORTER

The pain was too deep to the grave of her
emotions.
Deeper than Nebuchadnezzar's spouse watching
her grazing husband.
She couldn't handle it and neither could she cry
aloud.
Yes, she cried but her cheeks were dry.
The 'eye crevices' of her disturbed heart are the
ones that were tickled pink,
To produce a canal of tears!

Upon the middle of the night,
In deep sleep she seemed to walk forlorn,
Till cold winds woke her blue-eyed morn.
Her lonely ditched Grange could feel that
emotion ebb and flow,

That pushed her to drown into deep thoughts of
hurt or hate.
She only could say, "Love is Grim!"

Her moans bubbled with tears that rolled like
morning dew;
Like Cyrus weeping for his Persian Gulfport
war,
Her cries were bitter and cynical and icy!
She couldn't move- she had been hurt.
All could she do was hold the Messiah's
beautifying hand;
And find comfort and rest and consolation.

Fear still haunted her with his groggy sharp
claws;
And seemed crazy to pierce her wounds again.
She could not believe in any that attempted to
wipe her tears away.

The Comforter seemed so seductive in her eyes.

On a dark beach of reality versus confusion, she

was lying now.

With nothing to say but gobble up what had

been placed before her.

She couldn't scream!

She couldn't smile!

She could just drop teardrops

She couldn't move anything;

But her hand to hold on tightly onto the new

Romeo,

Who seemed so caring-Who wiped her tear

away!

©Ncube Tafadzwa

LIVING A LIE

This is the reality of life

It's getting more and tougher and tougher

We cry,we lie

We sigh,we discover

Yet we still play soft,

Seeing the truth but believe in lies .

It's the high time to differentiate between dreams

and reality

It's the high time to differentiate between

intelligence and education,

It's time to implement the lessons

Learnt from daily life sessions.and

Stop wishing for amnesia,

The voices in my head,

Mind full of dread

Waiting for the day

I end up dead

© Daisy Eripon

SUICIDE

Storms filled up my paradise,

A paradise that I thought I owned,

Life made of tears and pains

A peace that became pieces of my daily soul,

You may think I live that perfect life,

But the truth is

It's a shadow,of happiness

I'm a maestro of plastic life

Masking the dead living soul

.

Another day

Another cry

Another torture

Another lie

Another crying

Another dying

"Don't worry" " I'm fine"

I lie when they ask

" Don't worry I'll be alright"

I say as a year forms in the dark

" I'm not sad" I smile and say,

Faking the smile just to cover up the scar,

Suicidal thoughts runs in my mind

But to be honest,,

 Suicide doesn't fix things better

It only eliminates

It solidifies

Suicide justifies

Depression is a war

It hurts more and more

And expect to win,

I need a rest

A rest that I see no living

A rest that is eternal

Lord! Lord! Take my rest

I'm tired of the rest

©Daisy Eripon

REASONS WHY

The few that are genuine, I count you among

Compliments not like these I get

Getting over cruelty daily and mean

appreciations

You asked me to love my skin

Yea, I love it in pages, in novels, in volumes

But guess what

I can't tell the difference between a window and

a mirror

Because I look into both and see everything but

myself

Or see nothing but emptiness

You know that blinding feeling that comes

behind smiles and Positivity,?

That's what I hate, getting blinded,

Fooled by positivity and smiles,

By compliments, hugs and fake concerns

Today I will shine, but someone's shadow covers

me, I shine but not as bright

If it were the night, maybe it could be a lot like

the stars

I could get noticed if they took me into concern,

A concern that once am happy help me get

happy, coz it's for a moment

I hide the black to avoid hurting people,

But my own self is bruised,

That's how mean it is, to please others and kill

myself

I don't judge, I don't care about the world neither

But what if distance keeps me away from my

happiness

What if the karma you tell me about owns my

happiness

What if am just a mask of melanin but am white

on the inside

What if.

©Rose Pajero

NON FADING DARKNESS

I know what it's like to be addicted to pills

I do know what it's like to be an addict it kills

They say pain is a prison so let me out of my

cell

I sit in my room, tears running down my face

and I yell Into my pillowcases I cry out

I'm humiliated

I got this picture in my room and it kills me

Me happy and smiley

I feel like I lost something I never had

Happiness I mean, never had

Darkness has got me held captive You can see it

in my eyes

How it got my mind captured

I thought that maybe I'd feel better as time

passes

I know I said it would stop

But a couple weeks later am here singing the

same tune

I guess it has come back to finish me Crying my

eyes out in ink is difficult

But it's the only place that I can converse

Darkness took everything inside of me All I feel

is pain, pain that I can't walk away from

And back to my pills I go Therapy after therapy

not getting better

It's my new self

©Rose Pajero

DEAD BLACK WITH HATRED

An odd woman guided by feelings of pure

anguish ....tangled by hard facts ;

She feels naked _transparent _ shadowy !

Mixed images of fear relays like sand

through her clumsy memory box

She feels numb _slippery _bloggy !

All slippery like okra in a basin of Sadza -

Her thinking and feelings makes her

 choke with tightness ,

Her throat slackens

While her stomach burns with mere mockery ..!

A hazy black cloud of regret

shrewd within her !

Her teeth grits like ice age ..

Overtaken by tight feelings

as she lurks behind a curtain of indifference ...

Her holy of holies fragmented...

Her face broken into pieces by muffled hands !

Tears water eddies her eyes ...

An odd creature she endows

Blooming during the day

And ingloriously wilting during the night ...

She plays prey ..!

A nostalgic tone of beastly scenes shudders

In her haunting stomach ...!

Voices hum hauntingly

within the skeletons of her mind ..... !

Intensely she laughs with a ghostly tone

As if she is a reincarnated corpse !

Tears unscrew themselves from her iris ;

She stops still in the rewind ....

Burning liquid outflows

 from the gullies of her cheeks!

Aggressively she rubs it ...erasing _

the puffed make up on her oval face ;

Cotton tears ashen her face .....

Dead black with hatred

from the entangled web of imitation;

She feels ensnared _ tangled _embittered ;

She plays victim ..with three sulking kids and

nothing to raise the three

at the age of seventeen!

 burdening entrapments ,weak mists of

undivided pain .....child to child conceptions ..!

Butter her up ..raise her up from the scars of

unfreighted danger .. ...

Rehabilitate and groom her up ..

to be a wonder woman like us ....

For pain is her surname ...

Strap back she toils and moils over broken

knives ....

Give her light ..

Teach her to stretch out her wings and forge

forward ...!

©Chantelle Manesa